KEY
HUNTERS

THE
TITANIC TREASURE

KEY HUNTERS

*Getting lost in a good book
has never been this dangerous!*

KEY HUNTERS

THE
TITANIC TREASURE

by Eric Luper

Illustrated by Lisa K. Weber

SCHOLASTIC INC.

For Frank Hodge, champion of children's books and amazing guide to my journey

Text copyright © 2017 by Eric Luper.
Illustrations by Lisa K. Weber, copyright © 2017 Scholastic Inc.

This book is being published simultaneously in hardcover by Scholastic Press.

All rights reserved. Published by Scholastic Inc., *Publishers since 1920.* SCHOLASTIC, SCHOLASTIC PRESS, and associated logos are trademarks and/or registered trademarks of Scholastic Inc.

The publisher does not have any control over and does not assume any responsibility for author or third-party websites or their content.

No part of this publication may be reproduced, stored in a retrieval system, or transmitted in any form or by any means, electronic, mechanical, photocopying, recording, or otherwise, without written permission of the publisher. For information regarding permission, write to Scholastic Inc., Attention: Permissions Department, 557 Broadway, New York, NY 10012.

This book is a work of fiction. Names, characters, places, and incidents are either the product of the author's imagination or are used fictitiously, and any resemblance to actual persons, living or dead, business establishments, events, or locales is entirely coincidental.

Library of Congress Cataloging-in-Publication Data available

ISBN 978-1-338-14926-5

10 9 8 7 6 5 4 3 2 1   17 18 19 20 21

Printed in the U.S.A.   40
First printing 2017

Book design by Mary Claire Cruz

CHAPTER 1

When Evan opened his eyes, Cleo was beside him. They were lying on long wooden chairs, facing a railing that looked out on the sparkling night sky. The floor rocked gently as water rushed below them. The breeze chilled their cheeks, and Evan longed for the warm, welcoming fire of the magical library he and Cleo had found under their school.

But the last thing he remembered happening in the library was terrible, actually. Two trolls, Gary and Glen, had followed their master, George Locke, out of the last book he and Cleo had traveled into. The trolls had stolen their crystal key and given it to Mr. Locke. Then Locke had jammed the key into a new book, and everyone in the library had disappeared into its pages. Evan was growing used to the magic of the library, but the fact they were able to travel into actual books still amazed him. It frightened him, too. If they didn't finish the story in a book, they'd be trapped in it forever. But Evan and Cleo knew Mr. Locke was up to no good. Whatever he had planned, they couldn't let him win.

Cleo wore a dark dress under a frilly white apron. Evan looked down at himself. He had on a crisp white shirt and vest with a black bow tie.

"Where are we?" Cleo asked.

Evan stood and looked over the railing. Black water glided by far below. "I think we're on a ship."

"I think we're in trouble," Cleo said.

Evan followed Cleo's gaze. She was looking at a life ring hanging on the wall behind them. It read "RMS *Titanic*."

Evan's stomach did a flip-flop. He knew a lot about the *Titanic*. He'd read a book about it just a few months earlier. The RMS *Titanic* was a British ocean liner. On its first voyage it struck an iceberg and sank into the frigid waters of the North Atlantic. Of more than 2,200 passengers, only a few more than 700 survived.

"We've got to get off this ship," Evan said.

"We've got to get to the end of this story and find the key home before Locke does," Cleo replied. She and Evan were official Key

Hunters, and they had the necklaces to prove it. The fancy silver keys that hung from chains under their outfits meant they could enter any book in their magic library. But it didn't mean they could get back out!

"The end of this story is that the *Titanic* sinks to the bottom of the Atlantic Ocean. April 15 of 1912."

"There has to be something else," Cleo said. "Just like in all the other books we've traveled into. We have to figure out what problem needs to be solved and then go ahead and solve it."

Evan knew she was right, but how could he focus on solving problems when all he wanted to do was watch out for icebergs?

"There you are!" A deep voice boomed behind them. A ship's officer marched over.

His dark cap and the brass buttons of his uniform made him look like a train conductor.

"What are you two doing out here?" the man asked.

Evan and Cleo jumped to attention. "Just getting a breath of fresh air, sir," Evan said.

"You've got jobs in the First-Class Dining Saloon!"

"Our feet are tired from standing all day," Cleo said. "Our hands ache from . . ." She paused to think. "From whatever it is we do."

"That's no excuse," the officer said. "You're being paid two pounds a month to work on this ship. The White Star Line expects to get its money's worth."

Cleo leaned over to Evan. "How much is a pound again?"

"A little more than a dollar."

"Two dollars a month?" Cleo said. "I can find more than that between the seat cushions of my couch at home."

The officer stood tall. "That may be so, but if I don't see you both in the dining room in two minutes, I'll see to it that this is the last journey you ever make on the RMS *Titanic*."

"Somehow, I think it's the last journey any of us will be taking on the *Titanic*," Evan muttered.

The officer's face turned red. "What did you say?!?"

"Just that there are a lot of icebergs out there," Evan said. "Someone should warn the crew to watch out."

"We've got plenty of lookouts in the crow's nest," the officer replied. "Anyhow, the *Titanic* is unsinkable. There's no need to fear."

The officer marched off, and Evan and Cleo were left looking out at the ocean. The water had calmed, and now was so still they could see the reflection of the stars on the surface.

"We'd better get to work and figure out what we have to do in this story." Cleo looked over the railing. "We've got to stop Locke and his goons from doing whatever it is they have planned . . . and we have to do it before this whole ship ends up on the bottom of the ocean."

The dining saloon reminded Evan of his uncle Donnell's wedding. Comfy-looking chairs surrounded large tables draped in linen. Men wearing tuxedos and women in fancy dresses chatted over their meals. From the far side of the room, classy piano music floated to their ears.

"Keep your eyes open for Mr. Locke," Evan said.

Cleo started marching across the room. "I've found him."

A bearded man who could only be the ship's captain sat at a grand table. He wore a dark jacket with more brass buttons than anyone's. His chest was covered in medals and he had gold stripes circling his sleeves. A blond man with piercing eyes sat beside him. Even with a giant mustache, Evan could tell the blond man was Locke. Maybe it was the evil sneer. Gary and Glen sat at the table, too. They wore matching white sailor suits with shorts and shiny shoes. Each licked a giant rainbow lollipop.

"Those trolls might look cute if they weren't so ugly," Cleo whispered.

"Nothing could make those trolls look cute," Evan said.

Locke snapped his fingers. "Steward!" he called to Evan. "Refill our waters. Make it quick."

Evan hated serving Locke, but he might gather some clues if he stuck close. "Yes, sir," he said.

"Hey, your name must be Stewart," Cleo whispered.

"No, a *steward* is a waiter on a ship."

Evan grabbed a pitcher of water from a tray and began filling glasses. Cleo did the same.

"No spilling," Glen growled. His breath smelled like dead fish.

"More ice," Gary burped, dragging his slimy tongue across his lollipop. "More ice! More ice!"

"Yes," Locke said. "Bring us more ice. I understand the *Titanic* is equipped with one of those new ice-making machines."

The captain sat tall. "The RMS *Titanic* is equipped with every modern convenience."

"More ice! More ice!" Glen and Gary chanted.

The captain motioned to Evan and Cleo. "You'll bring two buckets of ice, one for each of these charming lads, thank you." He turned to Locke. "Now, what were you saying?"

Locke leaned in to speak to the captain. Evan folded a napkin nearby so he could hear. "I was wondering about books on board."

"We have a fine lounge right here in first class," the captain said. "There's also a library in second class. Both are well stocked with all the classics and some modern selections as well."

"Yes, I've had a look in both of those places. I was wondering about something a little more . . . unique."

"Well, there is the Rubaiyat," the captain offered.

"What's this Rubaiyat?" Locke asked.

"It's a jeweled book of Persian poetry. A collector in New York bought it at auction, and it's on its way to America. Perhaps I could arrange for you to have a look."

Locke grinned at Evan and Cleo. "That would be splendid. Books are so very interesting to me."

Evan darted out of the dining room.

"Where are you going?" Cleo struggled to keep up with him in her long dress.

"We need to get ice for the table," he said. "If we don't keep up our roles as stewards, who knows what will happen?"

Cleo stumbled. "What about that book?"

Evan stopped in the hallway. Other stewards rushed past carrying trays of beef and potatoes laid out on tiny plates. "I have a feeling that book is what Locke is looking for. If he's looking for it, we should be, too."

"Where do we start?" Cleo asked.

"We start by getting more ice." Evan said. "Then we have to search 883 feet of ocean liner."

CHAPTER 2

Even the hallways in first class were beautiful. Evan and Cleo rushed along the thick red carpeting, winding left and right.

"Where are you running off to?" Cleo said.

"We have to find the lounge," Evan answered. He knew Cleo was struggling in her dress, but it was nice to be the faster of the two of them for a change. "If we can't find anything there, we'll look in the Second-Class Library."

"But the captain said the Rubaiyat wasn't in either of those places."

Evan slowed to a fast walk and went up a flight of stairs. "If I've learned anything from being a Key Hunter, it's that libraries always have something to offer. Anyhow, Locke may not know exactly what he's looking for."

A huge room opened before them. The floor was spotted with small tables surrounded by green chairs. The air hung thick with stale cigar smoke, and a large chandelier hung from the ceiling. Nearby, a wall covered with shelves curved so they could see the spines of thousands of books. Evan sucked in a quick gasp.

"We don't have time to read all these books," Cleo said, walking up and down the shelves.

"If we're smart, we won't have to. Keep your eyes open for anything that looks strange."

"Everything looks strange. We're on one of the fanciest ships ever built." Cleo moved closer and whispered, "Plus, it's about to hit an iceberg and sink like a stone."

"Actually, it took a while for the *Titanic* to sink."

"How long is 'a while'?" Cleo asked.

"A few hours."

"Oh, that's a huge relief," Cleo said sarcastically.

"Well, at least once we crash we know we'll have some time."

"I'm going to use that time to find a life-boat and get off this ship."

Evan kept his eyes on the shelves. Each held hundreds of books bound in leather. Forest green. Midnight blue. Rich brown. Brick red. Some titles he'd heard of, some were new to him. He wanted to pull them all down and flip through the pages, but Cleo was right. It would take too long. Finally, his eyes rested on a thin book tucked between two fat ones. It was bound in leather like the rest, but something about it caught his eye: It was purple. It wasn't the bright purple their librarian, Ms. Hilliard, liked. It was more like eggplant. But it was the only purple book on all the shelves. Ms. Hilliard liked leaving them messages in purple.

Evan reached for the book, but Cleo's hand flashed past and snatched it. She laid it

flat on a nearby table and slid into one of the chairs. Evan sat beside her.

Gold letters stamped into the cover read:

MS. HILLIARD'S GUIDE TO ACCOUNTING, PLUMBING, AND COPPER MINING

Evan and Cleo glanced at each other.

"Why would Ms. Hilliard write a book about any of these things?" Cleo asked.

Evan shrugged. "Maybe it's a different Ms. Hilliard."

Cleo opened the book. The spine crackled as though the book had never been opened. The pages were covered in charts and numbers that made no sense to them.

Evan took the book and flipped through it. More boring charts and numbers.

"It's a purple book. Ms. Hilliard's name is

on the cover. This can't be a coincidence," Cleo said.

Evan looked more closely. The inside cover and the first few pages had numbers listed on them. Unlike the rest of the book, these numbers were bright purple. "Maybe this is something," he said.

The first line read:

DDC 813.3M   page 227   line 12   word 6

It went on like that, listing different numbers, pages, lines, and words. There were dozens of them.

"The page, line, and word numbers probably point us to words in these books that have to be put together to spell out a message," Evan said. "But what does the first number mean?"

"It's the Dewey decimal system!" Cleo exclaimed. "DDC stands for Dewey Decimal Classification. I remember it from the poster in our school library."

Evan's face went hot. He knew she was right and he was mad at himself for not figuring it out first. He leaped from his chair and scanned the shelves for the first book. When he found it, he pulled it out.

"*Moby-Dick*," Evan said. "The ship goes down at the end of that book, too."

"Then that's a good place to start." Cleo flipped to page 227. She scanned down the page. "Look, our names are here in the margin in purple ink. It's like Ms. Hilliard left us a sign that we're on the right track."

"What's the sixth word of line twelve?"

"If."

Evan's stomach flip-flopped. "It's going to take a year to figure out this message."

"We don't have a year," Cleo said. "But Ms. Hilliard wouldn't leave us a message if it wasn't important."

"And she wouldn't leave us a code we don't have time to figure out."

"Let's get to work." Cleo found pencils and paper on a nearby table. "I'll take the first half. You take the last."

"What if one of us grabs the books, and the other looks up the word? That way, we won't be bumping into each other when going to the shelves."

"Like a two-person assembly line," Cleo offered.

They set to work. Cleo found the books. Evan flipped through the pages and wrote down each word. It felt like they were work-ing for hours, but before long they had the full note. Evan read it aloud.

If you've solved this puzzle, you're on the hunt for the Jeweled Greats. Legend speaks of four important magical books. When brought together, these books will open doors never before opened to any librarian.

In the wrong hands, this power will bring great evil. In the right hands, it will bring great good.

The book on the *Titanic* is called the Rubaiyat, an ancient tome of Persian poems. The other three you'll have to discover.

But beware. Many librarians have tried to unite these books. None have ever returned.

Stay sharp!
Sandie Hilliard, librarian

Cleo started to say something, but a cough sounded from across the room. A figure darted from behind a heavy curtain and out the door. It was a girl.

Evan and Cleo glanced at each other in concern and chased after her.

CHAPTER 3

The girl was quick. They chased her through several corridors, down a flight of stairs, and along another hallway. As the girl turned the next corner, her foot hit the leg of a small table, and she tumbled to the ground at the edge of a high balcony.

As Evan struggled to catch his breath, he noticed the girl's torn overalls were a little too short in the legs. Her shoes had holes in them, and she wore a dark blue cap that covered red hair pulled into two braids. Soot smudged her cheeks.

"Why are you running away from us?" Cleo demanded.

Evan wanted to know the answer, but something else crossed his mind. "How are you not breathing hard?" he asked Cleo.

"Must be all the soccer, swimming, and lacrosse," Cleo said. "Trombone doesn't exactly help your cardio."

Evan wanted to tell her that playing the trombone improved lung capacity and music helped with math skills, but he knew this wouldn't impress her.

The girl rose to her feet. "We can't stay here," she whispered urgently. "We'll get in trouble."

They stood at the top of the most beautiful staircase Evan had ever seen. Polished oak railings led down to a landing where a clock was set into the wall. A glass dome above them shone light onto a lower staircase that swept forward to a tiled lounge where a bronze statue of an angel held a glowing torch. Spiral staircases on either side led to lower levels. Men and women in fancy clothes wandered in different directions. A few glared at the kids.

"Why can't we stay here?" Cleo said. "It's a nice enough place."

"That's the trouble," the girl said. "It's *too* nice."

"What's that supposed to mean?" Evan said.

"The Grand Staircase is for first-class passengers only," she said.

Evan's jaw clenched. He didn't like the idea that this beautiful staircase was open to certain people but off-limits to others.

"I'm Evan. This is Cleo," he said.

"My name's Elizabeth McManus," the girl said. "Everyone calls me Libby. My father is a fireman belowdecks, but he won't be for long if we don't get out of here."

"A fireman?" Cleo said. "How many fires need to be put out on a cruise ship?"

Libby shook her head. "A fireman tends the fire in a steam engine's furnaces. Mostly he shovels coal."

It seemed like a hard job to shovel coal all day. Hot, sweaty, and probably bad for your lungs.

"Follow me," Libby said. "I know this ship like the back of my hand."

"Just one second." Evan slipped down the stairs to the landing. The clock loomed above him. Two carved angels surrounded a round clock face that read eleven thirty.

"Do you know what today's date is?" he asked Libby.

She gave him a puzzled look. "It's April 14."

Cleo sighed in relief. "That gives us an extra day, Evan."

But Evan knew it didn't. The *Titanic* struck the iceberg just before midnight on the fourteenth and sank a few hours later on the fifteenth. They had only a few minutes.

"Let's go," he said. "We've got a lot of work to do."

Libby led them back down a hall and out a doorway to the deck. The cold air nipped at their cheeks.

"I heard you mention a jeweled book," the girl said. "The Ruby something?"

"The Rubaiyat," Cleo said.

Her eyes narrowed. "You're kind of young to be thieves."

"We're not thieves," Evan said. "We're trying to stop that book from being stolen by someone else."

"I wish I could help you." Libby sighed. "But I have troubles of my own."

Cleo walked alongside her. "What's the matter?"

"We're going to America to meet with my mother. She's already in New York. We couldn't afford to buy tickets, so my father agreed to work on the *Titanic* in exchange for our passage."

"That's good," Evan said.

"The trouble is a gold pocket watch has gone missing. One of the passengers in first class said he saw my father take it. Now my father and I will have to go back to England to stand trial."

"Well, did he take it?" Cleo asked.

"Of course not! The passenger who is accusing us is my mother's brother."

"Your uncle?" Evan said.

"Uncle Locke feels that a laborer like my father is no good for her. He's trying to keep us apart in the hopes my mom will remarry. I need to prove him wrong."

"Did you say Locke?" Evan said.

"Yes, why?"

"Does he have a bushy blond mustache?" Cleo asked as they made their way down the length of the ship.

"And nasty blue eyes?" Evan added.

Libby's stopped. "What's this about?"

"I think we may not have to go our separate ways after all," Evan said. "Locke is the one trying to steal the Rubaiyat."

Libby smiled. "It'll be nice to have some friends."

32

"And a partner who knows this ship," Cleo added. They all shook hands.

"So, what were you doing in the lounge?" Evan asked.

"I was looking for clues. The officers sometimes meet after dinner to unwind, and I thought I might overhear something useful. But then you came along talking about secret codes and a jeweled book."

"Do you know where the Rubaiyat is?" Cleo asked.

"No, but if it's of any value, it will be listed on the ship's cargo manifest. That's in the captain's cabin. It's risky, but I can take you there."

A crash sounded beside them. A deck chair splintered to pieces. More deck chairs began to shatter around them, followed by bottles, glasses, and a small table. Gary and Glen perched on the railing above. They were tossing down anything they could find. Their silly white sailor suits shone in the starlight.

"Cousin Gareth, Cousin Glenavan," Libby called out, diving aside to dodge another heavy chair. "What are you doing?"

"Stop Evan. Stop Cleo," they barked. "No get book!"

"That's Glen and Gary!" Evan said. He knocked aside a falling bottle. It flew over the railing and splashed into the water below. "They're creepy little trolls! Let's get out of here!"

The three kids ran toward the rear of the ship and up a metal staircase.

"Follow me," Libby said. "They won't follow us where we're going!" She grabbed the rungs of a ladder bolted to the ship's rearmost smokestack and started climbing. Cleo followed.

Evan paused. "Why do we always have to climb on our adventures?"

"Stop whining and look behind you!" Cleo called over her shoulder.

Glen and Gary were scurrying across the deck straight toward them.

Evan began to climb. The higher he went, the brighter the stars seemed to glow. He chanced a look down to see the trolls were still chasing them. Then everything began to spin.

Evan squeezed the rungs of the ladder. He heard a bell clanging, but wasn't sure if it was just his own heart pounding. "One step at a time," he told himself.

When he reached the top, the girls were sitting on the edge of the smokestack as if it was no higher than a porch swing. The stars shone more brilliantly than ever.

"Ready?" Libby said, motioning down into the smokestack.

"Won't we get burned alive in the coal tanks?" Evan asked.

"First of all, they're called furnaces," Libby said. "Second, the rearmost smokestack is just for show. It's not part of the engine."

A man's voice sounded in the distance. "Iceberg, right ahead!"

They looked toward the front of the ship. A white mass had appeared from the darkness.

"Oh no," Libby gasped.

The rear of the ship lurched to the right as the bow drifted left. The engines howled beneath them. At first it seemed the boat was

going to clear the iceberg, but then the screeching of twisting metal filled the air.

Chunks of ice showered the deck as the iceberg scraped along the right side of the *Titanic*.

The whole ship jolted. Glen and Gary fell from the ladder below. "Poor Glen! Poor Gary!" they hollered.

Then Libby, Cleo, and Evan fell into the darkness of the smokestack.

CHAPTER 4

As they fell, the only light came from the shrinking oval of stars above them. Evan flailed his arms, but he couldn't find anything to grab. Finally, he bounced across a cargo net that stretched above a churning engine. Cleo and Libby landed beside him.

"That . . . was scary," Evan said.

Cleo laughed. "That was fun!"

"I set up the net when I first discovered the

smokestack," Libby said. "It's faster than the stairs."

"You could have told us that," Evan said.

Libby smiled and slid down a rope. "I just did."

She opened a door and led them through a room filled with machinery. Huge gears spun in time with giant pistons that pumped up and down. It was too loud to talk—or even think—so they followed Libby to the next room.

Men scurried in every direction, shouting, pulling levers, and slamming furnace doors. Dark soot covered everything. Libby looked around until she saw a man with the same red hair she had.

"Father!" she called out. "Father, these are my friends, Evan and Cleo."

A smile flashed across the man's dirty face, but he quickly turned serious.

"Libby, something has happened to the ship," Mr. McManus said. "You need to find a safe place to wait until we fix things."

"Maybe we can help," Libby offered.

"This is no place for children."

A muffled voice came over a speaker as a metal door started lowering.

Libby's father kissed the top of her head. "The bulkheads are closing to protect the ship from flooding. Now go. I've got a job to do."

She gave him a quick hug. "Promise you'll find me."

"When in doubt, run uphill," said Mr. McManus. Then he turned away to tend to a furnace.

"Follow me!" Libby hollered as she ducked under the door.

Evan and Cleo trailed Libby through a series of rooms, each filled with workers running this way and that. Smoke filled the air. Water trickled down the walls. Doors lowered until they had to crawl under them to make it through. As they moved forward on the ship, the crew members seemed more and more panicked. Evan had to leap and dodge between them as they shut furnaces and worked water pumps.

"To the mail room!" Libby said.

"Mail?" Cleo said. "This is no time to send a postcard."

"There's a stairway in the mail room just next to the squash courts. It's the quickest way to the Officers' Quarters."

They raced through several more boiler

rooms. By the time they reached the mail room, water was pouring in through the wall. It was waist-high in some places. Some of the crew grabbed packages and stuffed them into canvas bags. Others hauled the bags to higher ground.

Libby jumped onto a chair, then to a long table. She ran along it and leaped to the staircase. Cleo and Evan followed. But as Evan ran, he got knocked over by a heavy mailbag and fell into the water. His eyes went wide. His spine went rigid. Cold like he had never felt before shocked through his body.

"Stop splashing around and come on!" Cleo shouted.

"I'm—I'm c-c-coming," Evan sputtered, leaping up.

He sloshed through the water and made

it to the staircase. Then the three kids clambered upward. Before long, their legs began to tire.

"How many floors does this boat have?" Evan complained.

"It depends where you are," Libby called over her shoulder. "Around eight."

"That's bigger . . . than most buildings . . . I've been in," Cleo said. Even she was losing her breath.

Libby led them back to the Grand Staircase. She paused to let Cleo and Evan catch up, then steered them up a fancy spiral staircase to the top of the ship. From there, they made their way to the deck outside.

The night was still. Evan looked for the iceberg in the distance, but it had disappeared as quickly as it had appeared. The ship tilted slightly forward and to the right. Behind him, passengers made their way to the railings and looked down at the water.

"There's no sign of any damage," one man said.

"I'm sure it was just a close call," another said.

Evan wanted to tell everyone to find life jackets, but he knew the crew would be coming around soon enough. If he and Cleo didn't find the Rubaiyat, they would fail in their mission and Locke would be closer to whatever awfulness he had planned.

They hopped over a low railing and slipped through a doorway into a long corridor.

"We're in the Officers' Quarters now," Libby whispered. "If we're caught, we'll be in big trouble."

They tiptoed along the hallway. They could hear the sound of men chattering.

Suddenly, a door swung open. An officer wearing a dark uniform rushed into the hallway. He looked them up and down with a sour face. "What are you doing here?"

Evan, Cleo, and Libby stood at attention.

"We weren't sure you were getting our messages from belowdecks," Libby said. "They couldn't spare any of the crew, so they sent me."

"We brought her up for a full report," Evan added.

The officer's jaw clenched. He was clearly unhappy that a girl in filthy overalls, a boy soaked to the bone, and a sweaty, panting girl were wandering around this part of the ship. "What can you tell us?"

"The hull has been breached," Libby said.

"The mail room and the squash courts are flooding," Cleo added. "The crew is doing their best to pump out the water, but—"

"The squash courts, you say?"

The three nodded.

"That information is useful. We can monitor flooding from the safety of the Viewing Gallery."

The officer turned and disappeared around a corner.

Evan, Cleo, and Libby crept farther along the hallway to a closed door.

"It's the Captain's Sitting Room," Libby whispered. "The cargo manifest should be somewhere inside."

"That will lead us to the Rubiayat," Cleo said as they slipped inside.

Dark paneling stretched from floor to

ceiling. Built-in drawers with brass handles and cabinets with glass doors lined the walls. A table stood in the center of the room and there was a desk in the far corner.

"This captain sure is tidy," Evan observed. "If this were my room—"

"Dirty socks would be everywhere," Cleo interrupted.

"That's exactly what I was going to say," Evan said.

"There's no time to lose," Libby said. "Let's find that manifest."

Evan felt guilty about searching the captain's private room, but it was the only way to stop Locke. He dug through a small pile of books on the desk while Cleo searched the drawers. Libby tugged open cabinets to check the shelves.

"I've got it!" Cleo pulled a leather book

from the top drawer nearest the captain's bedroom and flipped through the pages.

"Hurry," Evan said. "Find the Rubaiyat!"

But there was no time. The brass doorknob jiggled and the paneled door swung open.

CHAPTER 5

"Shhh!" Cleo put her finger to her lips.

Libby nodded. Evan stared at the ceiling, motionless. He clutched the cargo manifest to his chest.

The kids were lying side by side by side in the claw-foot tub in Captain Smith's private bathroom. It was a tight squeeze, but it was the only place large enough to hide all three of them.

"What if he comes in?" Evan mouthed.

Libby smiled. "They'll probably throw us overboard."

Captain Smith thumped around his room. He rifled through papers. He opened and closed a drawer. They heard him come closer.

Cleo's eyes were wide with panic. "Read the manifest."

Evan shook his head. "He'll hear me."

"We need to know where the Rubaiyat is in case he finds us." Libby snatched the book from Evan and flipped through the pages. She ran her finger down a column and then flipped through a few more.

Captain Smith cleared his throat.

They froze.

"Now, where did I put that manifest?" he muttered.

Evan poked his head up. The captain's back was to them. Evan grabbed the manifest from Libby and tossed it out the door onto the captain's bed. It bounced once and flipped faceup onto his pillow.

"Ah!" the captain said.

He picked up the manifest, shut off the light, and returned to his sitting room. Finally, they heard the door close and the sound of footsteps fading away.

Evan, Cleo, and Libby all exhaled at once.

"The book's gone!" Cleo said.

Libby leaped out of the tub. "Don't worry. I found it. The Rubaiyat is on E Deck. In the Quartermaster's Room."

With their mission accomplished, they slipped out of the captain's rooms and went back down the hallway into the cold night.

Passengers wearing puffy white life belts stood around nervously. A few men at the front of the ship kicked a lump of ice around the deck.

An officer pulled a tarp off a long lifeboat. "It's only a precaution," he reassured the passengers. "The captain wants us to be at the ready."

"Women and children first!" another officer called out.

Panic rolled through the crowd as people began to push forward.

Suddenly, the sound of a hundred train whistles blasted from the ship's smokestacks. Libby said something, but her voice was lost in the noise.

"What?!?" Evan screamed, covering his ears.

Libby came closer. Her face was ghostly

pale. "They're venting the steam from the engines!" she hollered. "Something must be really wrong!"

Cleo tugged Evan's arm and pointed to the men playing ice-soccer. "That man," she said. "He's got keys."

Evan looked. One of the men kicking at the ice wore a large ring of keys on his belt.

"If we get them, we can go home," Cleo said.

"But what about Locke and the Rubaiyat? What about Libby?"

"We're in a book," Cleo said in a hushed voice. "It's not even real. But if this ship goes down . . . well, who knows what'll happen to us?"

Evan thought about it. They'd been in a bunch of books so far, each more dangerous than the last. They had finished each challenge and done things he had never thought himself capable of. But this was the *Titanic*. There was no stopping it from sinking to the bottom of the ice-cold ocean.

He thought about his mom and dad, about his dog, Daisy. If Evan disappeared, who would scratch her in that spot behind her ear that made her leg kick?

"I do have a trombone recital tomorrow," he said.

"There's such a thing as a trombone recital?" Cleo asked.

"Just get those keys."

Cleo walked over to the men kicking the ice. "Excuse me," she said sweetly. "Would you mind lending me your keys for a few minutes?"

The man with the keys looked up. He put

his foot on top of the ice chunk. "And who might you be, lassie?"

"I'm Cleo. I'm a servant here on the *Titanic*."

"My name's Byron. I'm the best soccer player you've ever met." He smiled brightly. "And what would little Cleo want with the keys to every door on the ship?"

"A passenger is locked out of her cabin. She needs to fetch her coat."

"Sorry, lassie," Byron said. "I'd lose my job if the boss found out I'd given away my keys."

Cleo's eyes narrowed. She wouldn't be turned away so easily. "So, what are you doing over here?"

Byron kicked the chunk of ice back and forth between his feet. "Playing a bit of soccer. Now stand back before you hurt yourself."

"I've always wanted to play soccer," Cleo said. "But isn't it played with a ball?"

Evan smiled. Cleo was the best soccer player in school. She was pretending not to know about the game.

"It looks easy," Cleo added.

Byron chuckled. "It's not a sport for ladies."

Cleo took a step closer. "How about a wager then? If I score a goal on you, I get those keys."

Byron thought about it. "And what if I stop you?"

"What do you want?"

He kicked the ice chunk to Cleo. "How about a steak dinner from the kitchen?" He motioned to himself and his three friends. "One for each of us."

Cleo shook the man's hand and set up two deck chairs as a goal.

She hiked her skirt to her knees and planted her foot on the chunk of ice. "This won't be easy in high-heeled boots," she said.

"Feel free to back out."

"Not a chance." Cleo faked left and tapped the chunk of ice to the right. She scrambled her feet around and darted the other way. The chunk of ice seemed to dance across the deck. Byron moved closer. Evan was sure he was going to steal the ice chunk away. Then, Cleo gripped the ice between her ankles. With a flick of her hips, the chunk leaped into the air behind her. It lobbed over her shoulder and past Byron, who spun around and fell

down. Cleo slipped past and kicked the ice with the toe of her boot. It glided between the chairs and smashed against the ship's railing. Ice chips sprayed into the air.

Evan and Libby cheered. The man's friends laughed.

Byron stood and straightened his jacket. He unhooked the keys from his belt and placed them on a table. "You'd better return these soon."

"A deal's a deal." Cleo waved Evan over.

"Are you ready to get out of here?" she whispered.

Evan nodded. "One, two, three . . ."

They both touched the keys.

Nothing happened.

They touched the keys again. Cleo picked them up.

Nothing.

"I guess we do have to finish the adventure," Evan said.

Cleo gave him a worried look.

Finally, Libby snatched the key ring from both of them. "Let's go," she said. "There's no time to lose."

The boat was tilting more than before. Pulleys squeaked as the first lifeboat, less than half-filled, lowered to the water. A distress rocket fired into the air leaving a trail of white smoke behind it. It burst into brilliant sparkles.

Evan feared that Libby was more right than she knew. *There was no time to lose.*

CHAPTER 6

"Scotland Road?" Cleo called after Libby as they took the stairs two at a time. "We're like a thousand miles away from Scotland!"

"More like fifteen hundred," Evan panted.

"Scotland Road is the nickname for the long hallway on E Deck," Libby explained. "The Quartermaster's Room is on the port side of the hallway."

Cleo began to say something, but Evan cut her off. "When you're looking toward the front of the ship, port is to the left and starboard is to the right."

Libby came to the bottom of the stairs and rounded the corner. Crew members rushed along the hallway that stretched before them. It tilted to the right, and water trickled across the floor. When the lights flickered, Evan feared they would be lost in darkness. Libby rushed ahead, glancing at the brass plates on the doors. Finally, she stopped at one and jiggled the doorknob.

"Locked." Libby fumbled with the key ring and tried a few. None of them worked. "It'll take an hour to try them all!"

Evan took the keys and looked closely at them. In the dim light, he could make out letters and numbers stamped into the metal. "Libby, you said we're on E Deck, right?"

Libby nodded.

At the end of the hall, a door burst open and seawater began to flood in. Another door burst, this time closer. The cold water flowed around their ankles.

"Hurry!" Cleo threw her shoulder against the Quartermaster's door. It didn't budge.

Evan's hands shook. He flipped through the keys, looking for the letter E. He found ones stamped with B, C, and F. Another group was stamped ORL. Finally, he found a bunch marked E. He spun the keys around the ring, trying to make sense of the other numbers and letters.

By now the water was up to their knees.

"Hurry!" Cleo said, slamming into the door again.

He saw keys stamped with E-3rdCL,

E-Cook, E-2ndCL, and E-PurCl. None of it made any sense. Finally, he found a key marked E-QM.

"QM! Quartermaster!" He slid the key into the lock and twisted. The knob turned and the door opened. They sloshed down a hallway into a room lined with bunk beds. A bulb hung from the ceiling.

Suddenly, the whole ship groaned. The floor shook and shifted underneath their feet. The water level crept higher and the lightbulb seemed to swing toward the other side of the room.

"Quickly," Libby said. "The boat just leaned to port. This room will be filled in minutes."

They set to work, flinging open trunks and cabinets. Evan dug through rolled socks in a drawer. Cleo pulled several pairs of shiny shoes from a footlocker and tossed them into the water.

"Maybe the cargo manifest was wrong," Evan said.

"Or the book's been moved," Cleo suggested.

Libby flipped the mattresses off the bunks. "Or Locke got here first."

"I doubt it," Cleo said. "The door was locked."

By now the water was up to their thighs and rising quickly. Cold bit at them. The ship groaned again. Two more doors in the hallway burst open.

"We've got to get out of here!" Libby hollered.

Evan flung open the last cabinet. It held only dark uniform jackets and pants. "We've got to find that book!"

"Better off alive without it." Cleo moved toward the door. "Let's go."

Then Evan saw something. The green foam on top of the water was soaking the wallpaper. He could make out a dark rectangle behind one of the bunks. He waded over and felt along the edges.

"A secret panel!" he cried.

"Forget it!" Libby said. "It's just a book!"

But Evan and Cleo knew better.

Cleo came over and eyed the wall. She drew back a fist and punched it as hard as she could. The rectangle split into pieces. Cleo reached into the hole and pulled out a thick book. Hundreds of colorful gems were arranged on the cover to look like the feathers of three beautiful peacocks. The sparkling gems made the birds seem to dance.

Evan and Cleo took a moment to gaze at it, but were interrupted by another doorway bursting open in the hallway. The roar of the water rushing in the hall was almost deafening.

Libby grabbed Cleo and Evan. "Come on!"

They waded back to Scotland Road. Papers and trash littered the surface of the water. Libby pointed the way they had come and began to slosh along the long hall. "Father said to run uphill."

Cleo followed her. Evan tucked the book into his jacket and went after them. But as the water churned around them, it swept Evan off his feet. He went under, the cold numbing his fingers and stinging his face. Then the lights went out. Evan wanted to suck in air, but he knew better. He flailed his arms, searching for anything he could grab on to. He felt the wall sliding past. A pipe. The edge of a door. He needed to breathe. Badly.

Finally, someone grabbed his wrist and pulled. Another hand grabbed his sleeve. Soon his body heaved out of the rushing water, through a doorway, and onto a staircase.

He landed next to Cleo and Libby. The kids scrambled up the stairs and collapsed into a heap in a large kitchen. Evan coughed out salty water.

But there was no time to rest. The flicker of shadows on the wall told him they were not alone.

A man stood over them. It was Locke. Glen and Gary, still wearing their white sailor suits, hunched on either side of him.

Locke opened Evan's jacket and pulled out the Rubaiyat. "Thank you for finding my book," he said. A gold glint flashed as he placed the book inside his own jacket. "I should keep you around to find the other three Jeweled Greats. Soon, they will all be mine."

"Give it back," Cleo sputtered.

"Now, why would I do that, silly girl?" Locke said.

"Silly girl, silly girl," Glen and Gary repeated.

"Now, if you'll excuse me, we've got a life-boat to board," he said. "First class only, of course. Servants and steerage will have to wait their turn."

And with that, Locke, Glen, and Gary disappeared through the large, tilted kitchen and out a large, tilted door.

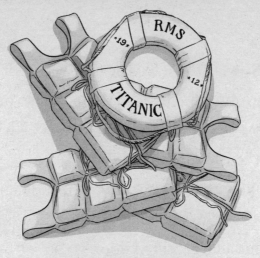

CHAPTER 7

By now, the front of the *Titanic* was underwater. On the deck, a small orchestra played soft music, but it did little to calm the passengers. Some argued near the lifeboats, which were being lowered to the dark water below. One lifeboat was nearly flooded by water being pumped from the side of the ship.

Libby pulled a blanket around her shoulders as she, Evan, and Cleo sat in wooden deck chairs. "Mr. Locke is gone. So is your book. And who knows where my watch is."

"We just need to figure out where Locke will go next," Evan said.

"He'll find a lifeboat, of course," a man sitting on a deck chair nearby replied. A woman sat next to him. They both wore bulky life belts around their waists. "Good evening. My name is Isidor Straus. This is my wife, Ida."

Evan, Cleo, and Libby introduced themselves. A violin's sad song filled the silence. Lifeboats drifted in the still water below, tiny dots in the distance.

"Why aren't *you* finding a lifeboat?" Evan asked him.

Mr. Straus wiped his glasses with a white cloth. "Women and children first. You three should find your seats. Boats are being lowered that aren't even full."

"What about you?" Cleo asked Mrs. Straus. "You're a woman."

The man shook his head. "My wife, Ida, she is very—"

Mrs. Straus squeezed her husband's arm and he stopped speaking. "We have lived together many years. Where he goes, I go."

Mr. Straus turned to his wife. "Ida, I beg you."

She smiled warmly. "'Many waters cannot quench love, nor can floods drown it.'"

He put his arm around her. Then he turned to the kids. "Why are you making the crossing to America?" he asked.

"I'm going to meet my mother," Libby said as another sparkly rocket fired into the air. "My father and I dream of America, where the streets are paved with gold. If we're allowed to stay, that is."

"Gold only comes to those who work hard," Mr. Straus said. "But it's true that America offers opportunity to those willing to work for it. This is not true in many other places."

Evan never thought about it much. His parents worked hard, but they had a lot of opportunity, too. He went to a good school. They lived in a nice house and had all the food they wanted. He and Daisy had a big yard to run around in. He never worried about much of anything. The idea that other people did worry about those things made him feel bad.

"My husband, Isidor, started off selling china in a store in New York City," Mrs. Straus said proudly. "Now, we own R. H. Macy and Company."

"You own Macy's?" Cleo said. "The department store chain?"

"Chain?" the man laughed. "We have only one location. Herald Square in Manhattan."

But the word "chain" was already getting Cleo's brain whirring. "I saw it," she whispered. "The pocket watch. Locke was wearing it."

Libby sat up. "Uncle Locke has it? I can't believe he'd frame my father! But he wouldn't be so brazen as to wear it in the open, would he?"

"I'm not sure what *brazen* means," Cleo said, "but I know what I saw. The chain stretched right across his belly. It was a gold pocket watch."

"If everyone is looking to get on a lifeboat, then Locke will be there, too," Evan said. "Let's go."

They said their good-byes to Mr. and Mrs. Straus and ran off.

They searched along the sloping deck, but couldn't find Locke anywhere. At the rear of the ship, a group of passengers huddled against the railing. Evan, Cleo, and Libby pushed through the crowd but they didn't recognize anyone.

"Maybe he went back belowdecks," Cleo suggested.

"Why would he do that?" Evan whispered. "Locke would only need to get into a lifeboat and watch the ship go down to finish out the story."

"Well, he isn't anywhere around here," Cleo said.

Suddenly, Libby pushed past them. "Father!" she cried out.

Mr. McManus stepped out of the crowd and swept Libby up in his arms. He was covered in soot, but neither of them seemed to care. "I thought I'd never see you again."

"Oh, Papa, you can't get rid of me that easily." Libby turned to Evan and Cleo. "My friends and I have been chasing after Uncle Locke."

Libby's father's face turned serious. "Stay away from him. He's a bad man."

"I know," Libby said. "Not only did he steal that pocket watch you were accused of taking, but he stole a book Evan and Cleo need."

"Plus, Gary and Glen smell like dead fish," Cleo mumbled.

"Forget about the pocket watch, forget about your book. The damage to the ship is too great. The lower decks are flooded. The *Titanic* is sinking. There's no saving her. All three of you need to get onto lifeboats."

"But Mother is waiting for us in America," Libby said. "The pocket watch will—"

Mr. McManus gave them all stern looks. "Nothing is more important than your lives. Find lifeboats. Save yourselves."

Libby started to argue, but her father put two fingers over her lips. "Libby, they are taking women and children. There's no way they'll let a coal shoveler like me on board. First class, second class, even third class goes before I do. Get on a lifeboat. I'll find another way."

"Daddy, no!"

"Do what I tell you, child. Nothing's going to stop me from finding you." He hugged Libby and then thrust her toward the crowds gathered around the railings. "Now go!"

The closer they got to the lifeboats, the more people pushed and shoved. Men shouted and argued. Shipmates struggled to keep order as a lifeboat was being lowered from the deck.

Evan looked down. Two homely kids in white sailor suits grinned up at him.

Cleo pointed at them. "Glen and Gary!"

"Toodle-oo!" they called.

Gary tugged at the hem of a woman's dress. A hand fan covered most of her face, but Evan recognized the piercing, evil eyes peering over it.

"Locke!" Evan shouted. "He dressed as a woman to get on a lifeboat!"

Locke's eyes twinkled and he gave a wink. The jeweled Rubaiyat sparkled from under one arm. Then, the "woman" sat down on the bench and turned away. Evan climbed the rail ready to jump, but the lifeboat was too far away.

One of the shipmates pulled Evan down. "Hold your horses. There are more lifeboats on the starboard side. We'll find you a seat."

But Evan darted toward the stairs.

"Where are you going?" Cleo yelled after him.

"Locke is down there. He's got the book. He's got the watch!"

Evan raced down the stairs, the steps uneven under his feet. He looked out every window he passed. The lifeboat was still far below. The metal bones of the ship groaned as the *Titanic* took on more water. A door led to a lower deck, but it was locked.

There was only one thing to do. Evan sprinted outside and leaped over the railing into the darkness.

CHAPTER 8

Evan hated heights. He hated feeling out of control. But he knew the rules of being a Key Hunter. If Locke got away with the Rubaiyat and found the key to get out of this book, he and Cleo might be stuck inside its pages forever. For most people on the *Titanic*, forever meant the bottom of the ocean.

As Evan flailed through the air, the black ocean grew closer. Then his hand hit a rope. He grasped it and swung toward solid wood where he fell against someone's legs. He was in the lifeboat!

Locke shrank back, clutching the Rubaiyat to his chest. The fan still covered his face. Glen and Gary lunged forward and began hitting Evan with their giant, rainbow lollipops.

"That boy!" Locke screamed in a high-pitched voice. "He's trying to steal my family's treasures!"

Two crew members grabbed Evan by his jacket. One of them was Byron, the man Cleo had played ice-soccer with.

Gary stomped on Evan's foot. "We lose. You win," he growled.

"You mean, 'You lose. We win,'" Glen said.

"Whatevers."

The Rubaiyat sparkled in the light of the

ship. Evan glanced up to see Cleo and Libby hanging over the railing of the lowest deck. Cleo was reaching for him.

Evan knew what he needed to do. In a flash, he slipped his arms from his jacket, and pushed past Gary and Glen. Then he snatched the Rubaiyat from Locke, took a running jump off a bench, and leaped toward the *Titanic*. With the book in one arm, he wasn't sure he'd have the strength to pull himself onto the deck, but he couldn't leave Cleo and Libby behind. The *Titanic* had only moments before it would sink to the bottom of the Atlantic. They'd have to figure something out fast.

Cleo grabbed Evan's outstretched hand. He swung down and slammed into the hull of the ship. His breath burst out of his lungs.

"Give me your other hand!" Cleo said.

"The book . . ." Evan coughed. His hand slipped a little.

"Forget it," Cleo said.

But he couldn't. Evan twisted. He flung the book up. It landed on the edge of the deck. Libby snatched it. Evan thrust his free hand into Cleo's, and she hauled him on board.

"There's no time to catch your breath," Libby said. "We have to run."

"Why?" Evan panted.

Libby pointed over the railing. Gary and Glen were climbing the ropes that held the lifeboat, lollipops clutched in their teeth.

Locke's eyes blazed. He dropped his fan and pointed at Evan.

"That's no woman!" a lady on the lifeboat hollered. "He has a mustache!"

"The scoundrel did it to get a seat on the lifeboat!" someone else shouted. "Get him!"

Locke hopped to the edge of the lifeboat and began climbing the rope. Byron tugged at Locke's skirt, but it tore off to reveal pink frilly bloomers with daisies on them. Locke kicked off the skirt and continued to climb.

Evan, Cleo, and Libby didn't stick around. They weaved through a lounge and along a hallway, making several turns until they came upon a staircase. Libby started down.

"Your father said, 'Always head uphill!'" Cleo said.

"Locke will expect that," Libby said. "Anyhow, I'm the daughter of an engineer. I'm more comfortable down below."

Evan knew the ship was filling with water fast. He also remembered that in its last moments, the rear of the *Titanic* rose out of the water until the boat couldn't handle the weight and split in two. Then it was only a few minutes until the whole ship plummeted more than two miles to the seafloor.

"No way," Evan panted.

But the argument ended suddenly when Locke charged into the hallway with Gary and Glen close behind.

"This ends now," Locke said. "Give me the book."

"Give us the pocket watch," Cleo said. "Even trade."

"That's actually fair." Locke patted his pockets, but he had none. His skirts were back on the lifeboat. "I seem to have lost it." He turned to Libby. "Looks like you and your wretched father will be headed straight back to England after this disaster."

Evan looked down the staircase. Water

was quickly rising from below, but he could see a doorway under the surface. "Then it looks like you'll have to do without the Rubaiyat."

Evan grabbed the book and dove into the icy water. Libby and Cleo plunged in after him. The water felt colder than before, and it took a few seconds for Evan to get his arms and legs moving. Some lights were still working, which gave the water an eerie, green glow. He swam through the doorway and found an air pocket. His head bobbed close to the ceiling. His breath was short and choppy.

Libby's head poked up next to him. Her hair lay flat against her forehead.

"Where's Cleo?" Evan asked.

"I don't know. The last thing I saw was those two brats coming after us!"

Evan worried that Cleo was trapped some-where under the water. He turned to go back, but Gary appeared, spitting out a mouthful of seawater.

"We get you," he growled. "We get you good!"

Hands grasped at Evan's foot. Glen was pulling him under!

Tightening his grip on the soaking-wet book, Evan kicked free, and dove under the water. He swam away from the terror twins and found another pocket of air in the next room. Libby came up alongside him. Evan knew he wouldn't last long in water this cold, but he had to keep moving. He and Libby made their way from room to room until they found a ladder leading up to a higher level.

Libby started climbing.

"What about Cleo?" Evan shouted.

"She's a smart girl. She'll find her own way out."

It was the first time he and Cleo had been separated in a book, and Evan wasn't sure what that meant. Could a Key Hunter be in one part of a book while another was somewhere else? He glanced over his shoulder, but saw only two lollipops sticking up from the water. They drifted closer like rainbow shark fins.

The lights flickered. Then everything went dark.

Evan felt for the ladder and climbed after Libby.

"You'll never get the Rubaiyat!" Cleo hollered over the sound of rushing water. It rose around her ankles to her legs. She tugged at her skirt, but it was caught on the staircase's wooden banister.

"I don't need it," Locke said calmly.

Cleo froze. "But . . . I thought . . ."

"You thought getting the Rubaiyat was the goal. Silly girl. As long as I get out of this book, I can come back anytime to get that Jeweled Great." Locke came to the top of the tilting stairs. He looked down at Cleo. "And it will be much easier once I get you and your pesky friend out of the way."

The water rose above Cleo's waist. "You wouldn't leave us to sink to the bottom of the ocean."

Locke smiled evilly. "It's part of the magic of books," he said. "You're just servants here. No one will miss you. But I'm the main character. The main character always wins."

Locke turned and sloshed away.

Minutes passed, and the water level rose past Cleo's shoulders. She pulled on her skirt, but it wouldn't tear. The ship groaned again. Cleo took a deep breath as her head sunk below the surface.

CHAPTER 9

Cleo needed to breathe. She felt along the banister until she found the spot where the fabric of her skirt was stuck. It was wedged in tightly. She planted her foot on the carved wood and kicked. *THUMP.* She kicked again. *THUMP!* The banister began to split. Her lungs begged for air and her back ached from pulling, but finally she heard a loud *CRACK!*

Cleo swam upward. When her head burst above the surface, she sucked in a deep breath.

The cold numbed her arms and legs, but she paddled to the stairs and began to climb.

"Uphill," she told herself. "Run uphill."

Evan searched the crowd huddled at the rear of the *Titanic*. They were as "uphill" as they could get, but there was no sign of Cleo anywhere. He called out her name. Libby did the same.

An old woman came over. "It's all right, sweeties," she said, pulling her shawl around her shoulders. "It will all be over soon."

"No it won't," Libby said. "My mother is waiting for me in America. That's where it all begins!"

Just then, the deck bucked under their feet, and the rear of the *Titanic* began to rise quickly out of the ocean. One of the ship's smokestacks twisted free and crashed into the water. Screams rose from the lifeboats below as the passengers rowed away from the sinking ship.

"Cleo!" Evan screamed, clutching the railing. "Where are you?"

Suddenly, a set of double doors burst open and Cleo scrambled up the deck. Her dress was soaked and sagging. "Where's Locke?" she hollered. "If he finishes this story without us, we're stuck!"

"This book doesn't end until the *Titanic* is underwater," Evan said.

"I'm not sure what you mean about stories and books," Libby said, "but the *Titanic* is going to be underwater sooner rather than later!"

All at once, the ship snapped across the middle, and the rear of the *Titanic* dropped. Great walls of water splashed around them. Screams filled the air. Evan and Libby clutched the railing, while Cleo fell to her hands and knees and crawled toward them.

As the front end of the ship sank, it began to lift the rear higher again. The deck grew steeper and steeper. Tables and chairs slid toward the sea. Two men lost their grip and fell into the water. Cleo scrambled closer and, with one final leap, reached for Evan and Libby.

Evan stretched as far as he could and grabbed her wrist. Libby hung from the railing by one arm and helped pull Cleo to their side.

"The Rubaiyat," Cleo said to Evan.

"I've got it." He held up the book. The pages were soaked and the binding was torn. Some of the gems were missing from the cover.

Cleo wrinkled her nose. "Can you still call that a book?"

Evan shrugged. "It's a drippy book."

The *Titanic* began to sink faster. The rear half of the ship was sliding quickly into the water. It would be only moments before the ship disappeared completely. Evan had no idea what to do next. He glanced at Cleo and Libby, but they looked just as helpless.

Then someone snatched the book from Evan's hand. It was Glen! His sailor suit was dirty and wet. He tossed the Rubaiyat to Gary, and they hopped over the railing into the darkness. Evan pulled himself up and leaped after them. He didn't know what to do about a sinking ocean liner, but he did know what to do about these trolls.

SPLOOSH!

The water was colder than ever. He paddled away from the sinking ship, thankful for the swimming lessons his parents forced him to take when he was five. The *Titanic* roared behind him as it sank. Air rushed out the windows and doors of the upper levels. Glass shattered and steel groaned.

Evan kept paddling. He saw a flash of white. Gary's shirt? He swam toward it, his body shivering and his muscles cramping from the icy water.

Just as he was about to give up, Evan felt a foot. He tried to grab it, but it kicked away. He swept his hand around in the water and felt it again.

"*My* book!" Gary growled, his meatball head bobbing above the water. "*My* book!!"

Evan pulled Gary close and yanked the Rubaiyat from the little troll's hands.

But that's when Glen pounced. "My book! My book!! My book!!!"

Glen and Gary swatted Evan, their lollipops two round blurs of rainbow sweetness. Evan's arms and legs grew weak, and he began to sink. His head slipped beneath the water. Two miles of frigid water separated him from the bottom of the Atlantic.

Suddenly, an arm looped around his waist and pulled him toward the surface. It was Cleo! She kicked her legs and brought them up for air. They sucked in deep, shivering breaths as a sailor hauled them into a lifeboat. Evan saw some of the same faces from the lifeboat he'd been on earlier.

"Ah, my little ice-soccer partner. It would be a shame to lose a talent like yours."

"B-B-Byron." Cleo shivered. "I th-think I lost your k-keys."

Byron wrapped Cleo in his coat. "Somehow, I don't think I'll be needing them anymore, lassie."

A woman handed Evan a blanket, and he and Cleo huddled together on the floor of the boat. Locke, Glen, and Gary sat across from them on benches. Locke stared at Cleo and Evan with laser-beam eyes.

"Where's the book?" Cleo whispered.

"I must have dropped it in the water."

Cleo's eyes filled with fear. "So, what do we do now?"

Evan thought about his parents. And Daisy. The idea that he may never see them again made him want to cry. The only way he knew to deal with it was to make a joke. "I guess we get used to life without television?"

Cleo pulled Byron's coat around herself and turned away. Evan could tell she was also trying not to cry.

Just then, a hand grabbed the side of the lifeboat. The men pulled in another figure. It was Libby! She rolled onto her back, clutching the Rubaiyat to her chest.

"That girl is nothing more than a common thief!" Locke hollered. "First she stole Mr. Straus's gold watch, and now she has my book!"

"She's no thief!" A man who was also soaked to the bone rushed to Libby from the rear of the rowboat. It was Mr. McManus.

"P-p-papa, I thought I'd l-l-lost you," Libby managed to say through chattering teeth.

He hugged her tightly. "You can't get rid of me that easily, my treasure."

Locke's torn skirt lay in a heap on the floor. Evan grabbed it to wrap around Libby. He felt a lump inside. He reached into a pocket and pulled out a gold pocket watch. Even in the darkness, it glinted in the starlight. The inscription read:

For Izzy,
My love for you reaches any depth.
Eternally yours, Ida

"There must be some mistake," Locke said, standing. "That watch . . ."

"That watch was in the pocket of *your* skirt," Cleo said accusingly.

The crew members grabbed Locke by the shoulders and sat him back down.

"I'm not sure what game you're playing at," Byron said, "but I'm sure the police will want to speak with you once we're rescued."

As far as Evan knew, all the lifeboats that escaped the *Titanic* were saved. It was good to know because everyone they had met on their adventure was aboard. Well, almost everyone. Evan looked out at the water. A few deck chairs floated by. He wondered if Isidor and Ida had made it onto one of the other lifeboats.

"Thank you so much for helping me find that watch," Libby said through blue lips. "Maybe we can stay in America after all."

Libby's father clutched her tightly, rubbing her back to warm her.

Evan held out the watch. The chain dangled. At the end hung an ordinary, brass key with the word MACY'S stamped into it. Evan and Cleo glanced at each other. Locke lunged forward. Gary and Glen reached for it.

All at once, letters burst from the key like a thousand crazy spiders. The letters tumbled in the air around them and began to spell words. The words became sentences, the sentences paragraphs. Before long, they could barely see through the letter confetti until everything went black.

CHAPTER 10

The warmth of the library fireplace did little to thaw Evan and Cleo. Their limbs were numb from swimming in the North Atlantic. As they held their hands out to the flames, they rubbed their palms together and wiggled their fingers until some of the feeling came back. The magic library under their school was just as they had left it. Locke, Glen, and Gary were nowhere to be seen. Evan and Cleo were back in their school clothes, as dry as when they had entered the book.

The Rubaiyat sparkled in the flickering light. It was dry, too. The cover was no longer torn or missing any of its twinkling jewels. Evan picked it up. There was nothing more beautiful to him than a brand-new book—the crackling binding waiting to be opened, the crisp pages begging to be turned. He inhaled deeply. The Rubaiyat gave off the scent of salt water, reminding him of his time on the *Titanic*.

Cleo rubbed her hands up and down her shoulders. "So what do we do now?"

"Do you think the school nurse knows how to treat frostbite?"

"I mean with the Rubaiyat. We can't just stick a treasure like this in our backpack."

Just then, a glass case rose from the floor. It reminded Evan of something he might see in a museum. Inside stood four small pedestals, each empty.

"Four Jeweled Greats. Four pedestals . . ." Evan said. "Do you think . . . ?"

"Of course I think," Cleo said. She took the book and placed it in the case.

The glass shut and a light shone from above. The Rubaiyat glittered more brightly than ever.

"Three more to go," Cleo said. "What do you think happens once we find them all?"

"Ms. Hilliard said it will open doors never before opened to any librarian."

"But what does that mean?"

Evan thought about it. "No idea."

As they made their way up the stairs, Cleo pulled something out of her pocket. It was

the brass key they had found on the life-boat, the one that brought them home. It was attached to a chain. At the end hung the gold pocket watch.

"What do we do with it?"

Evan shrugged. "Right now, I just want to go home and sleep for a month."

Cleo laughed. "I might sleep for two months."

Upstairs in their school library, they found Mr. Locke scanning books at the front desk. Glen and Gary were sliding a ladder along the aisles, returning books to the shelves.

"Ah, Evan! Cleo!" Mr. Locke said. "Glad you're enjoying your time in the library."

Evan and Cleo glanced at each other. Why was Locke being so friendly?

"I spoke to Principal Flynn," he said. "When I told her how much you both love it here, she agreed to have you join me for recess *and* free period. Maybe we can arrange for you to come in on the weekends as well."

"Uh, I'm not sure we can . . ." Evan started.

"Of course you can," Mr. Locke said. "After all, every moment you spend out of the library is a moment lost."

Locke leaned in close and whispered, "The two of you proved quite helpful in getting me the first of the Jeweled Greats. I'm sure you'll be just as useful finding the next one."

Cleo folded her arms across her chest. "Why would we help you?"

Mr. Locke leaned back in his chair. "I think this may convince you." He slid a note across the desk. It was written in purple ink on lavender paper.

Dear Evan and Cleo,

One of the benefits of being a sorceress in a fantasy novel is that I can use my magical mirror to watch your adventures from my royal palace in the trees. You did an amazing job aboard the *Titanic*. I couldn't be more proud.

Sometimes in life we need to do things that require unusual bravery. Policemen and fire-fighters, for example, must charge toward danger instead of running away from it. I need you both to be brave.

I'm not sure which book your key will bring you into next, but it is important you take on this challenge. Locke will no doubt try to find a way in. However, if you complete any of these adventures without him, he will not be able to control the Jeweled Greats. That power will be yours alone.

You've already shown great bravery. Stay on your path and you will accomplish incredible things.

Yours truly,
Sandie Hilliard, librarian

Evan warmed at the thought of Ms. Hilliard watching their adventures, but hated the idea that he and Cleo would have to work with someone as nasty as Locke. He slid the note back across the desk.

"We'll be here after school tomorrow."

Locke smirked. "Excellent. Now run along. And be sure to get a good night's sleep. I look forward to our partnership."

Gary and Glen began hopping up and down on their ladder. "Partners! Partners!!

Partners!!!" Gary lost his footing and fell to the carpet, sending Glen into a burst of giggles.

Evan and Cleo walked out of the library into the busy hallway. Students zipped past as they made their way to class.

"I can't go on an adventure after school tomorrow," Cleo told Evan. "I have soccer practice."

"You sure you need to practice?" he asked. "You did a great job against Byron on the deck of the *Titanic*."

"Evan, no matter how good you are you *always* need to practice."

"Don't worry," he said. "Our adventure won't *be* after school. We're going into the next book early tomorrow morning. We'll go in without Locke and get the second Jeweled Great ourselves."

"Sneaky, sneaky," Cleo said, patting her pocket. "I'll see you there with the key to our next adventure."

And with that, she disappeared into the sea of students.

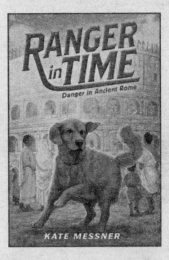

JOIN THE RACE!

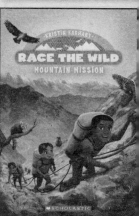

It's an incredible adventure through the animal kingdom, as kids zip-line, kayak, and scuba dive their way to the finish line! Packed with cool facts about amazing creatures, dangerous habitats, and more!

■SCHOLASTIC

scholastic.com

RAC